WISHING WELLNESS

A WORKBOOK
for Children of Parents with Mental Illness

by Lisa Anne Clarke
illustrated by Bonnie Matthews

MAGINATION PRESS • WASHINGTON, D.C.

**This book is intended to be used by children
only with the direct supervision of a therapist,
other mental health professional, or adult caregiver.
For therapists and others using this book in their work
with children, please see the comprehensive
Therapist Resource Guide available online at
http://www.maginationpress.com/441A313.html.**

Published by
MAGINATION PRESS
An Educational Publishing Foundation Book
American Psychological Association
750 First Street, NE
Washington, DC 20002

For more information about our books, including a complete catalog, please write to us,
call 1-800-374-2721, or visit our website at www.maginationpress.com.

Book design by Susan K. White
Printed by Worzalla, Stevens Point, Wisconsin

10 9 8 7 6 5 4 3 2 1

*This book is dedicated to the many children
who have a parent suffering from mental illness,
and especially to Jeweleah.
In memory of Ralph and Violet* – LAC

*To Amy Telep Dibos, for all of her work with children,
young adults, and women* – BM

CONTENTS

CHAPTER 4

CHAPTER 5

CHAPTER 6

Introduction

This workbook was written for young people like you who have a parent with a mental illness. This book is meant to be shared with someone such as a therapist or counselor who is helping you learn about and deal with your parent's illness.

It can be very hard for kids when a parent has an illness of any kind, but it's especially hard to have a parent struggling with serious mental health problems. Most young people don't know very much about mental illness. When you don't know enough about your parent's illness or about what's happening, things can seem very confusing. Sometimes they can even seem scary.

This workbook will help you understand mental illness and sort out the facts from false information. It explains what causes most mental illness and how doctors can help people with mental illness get better. The drawing and writing activities can help you understand your feelings and worries, and help you share them with someone you trust.

This book will also help you feel better about your parent. And most of all, it will help you feel good about yourself!

CHAPTER 1

YOUR PARENT'S MENTAL ILLNESS AND YOU

Let's start by thinking about yourself and your family. In this chapter, you are invited to think back to what you first thought and felt when you found out about your parent's mental illness.

Here you have a chance to think about what you already know about mental illness too. You can share this information with the person who is helping you read this book. This can help him or her get to know you better and figure out what you want to know.

This chapter will also help you understand a bit more about how our minds work and how mental illness can sometimes change the way your parent thinks, feels, and behaves. It will also give you an idea of what you can expect to learn in the rest of this book.

ABOUT ME

My name is_____.

I am_____years old.

I am in the_____grade.

This is a book about me, my parent, and what I'm learning about mental illness.

I am working on this book with

_____, who is my_____.

This is me.

Draw a picture or paste a photo of yourself here.

MY FAMILY

My mom's name is_____.

My dad's name is_____.
This is a drawing of my parents.

This is my family tree.

Fill in the names of all your family members in the spaces above.

My_____has a mental illness.

The mental illness is called_____.
Lots of people have this kind of mental illness.

Sometimes mental illness can make it very hard for people to think clearly. Mental illness can make people *feel* differently too sometimes. Of course, no one feels happy all the time, but people with mental illness might feel extra sad, mad, scared, excited, or even giggly. Mental illness can also cause people to behave in ways that are hard for others to understand.

Sometimes I think my parent feels like this:

Sometimes my parent behaves like this:

If you are like most kids who have a mom or dad with mental illness, you probably don't like some of the things your parent does or says. Kids often say they hate their parent's mental illness but love their parent. They know their parent doesn't want to be ill. Kids know their mom or dad is trying hard to be a good parent. Like them, you probably hope your parent will get better soon, and you feel bad when he or she is ill.

If only just wishing could make them well—for always!

How Our Minds Work

Understanding mental illness can be hard for anyone— even grown-ups. To help you understand, let's talk about how you use your thoughts and your imagination.

Do you know what imagination is? Maybe you've pretended that you were a king or queen living in a beautiful castle, or a firefighter putting out a raging blaze in a forest, or an astronaut traveling to the moon. These things aren't really happening, but you can use your mind to imagine interesting things to think about and fun ways to play. You can even wish that what you imagine may come true some day.

Here are some fun things I've pretended or imagined:

Dreaming and Your Imagination

If you're like most people, you can remember some of the dreams you've had while sleeping. While you're sleeping, your mind uses your imagination to dream without you telling it to. Your mind just does it automatically. These dreams can seem very real! When you're dreaming, you often think the dream is really happening.

When you are awake, it's different. When you're awake, you can tell your mind when to imagine and when not to. But when you're asleep, you can't control your imagination.

Some of our dreams are scary...

and other dreams are nice.

The best dream I can remember is:

In some ways, serious mental illness is a little like dreaming. Most people with serious mental illness have some trouble controlling their imagination and knowing what is real or true all the time.

People with serious mental illness might have lots of mixed-up thoughts or emotions that make them feel confused, scared, angry, or sad. They don't understand that their brain isn't working properly, and they can't understand what is really happening around them. They may confuse what people say or do. They may act in strange ways others don't understand because others don't know what they are imagining. Or they may imagine something is happening that really isn't. They might think they can hear noises or voices or see things that aren't really there.

Your parent might say or do something that makes you know he or she is imagining things. Your parent may not understand something that happened or may not be able to make sense of something you said. Has this happened to you? How do you know when this happens?

I know my parent is ill when:

Sometimes my parent sees or hears things
that aren't real, such as:

FINDING OUT ABOUT MY PARENT'S ILLNESS

The way I found out about my parent's illness was:

I was_____years old.

At first, I wasn't sure what was happening, but I felt like something was wrong. I thought:

When I was told that my parent had a mental illness, I thought:

This is what I know about my parent's illness now:

This is what I want to learn from this book:

CHAPTER 2

THE SIGNS AND TREATMENT OF MENTAL ILLNESS

In this chapter you will learn about all the different signs of mental illness that people who are ill sometimes have or show. It is very unlikely that any one person has all of the possible signs, which are also called symptoms.

This chapter also tells you the meaning of many words you may hear adults use to describe your parent's signs.

And perhaps most important, it gives some basic information about the treatment of mental illness that most people receive. If you would like to know more about the treatment your own mom or dad is getting, ask the person helping you with this workbook or your family doctor for answers to your questions.

Mental Illness and the Brain

Mental illness can affect the part of people's brains that controls their thinking, imagination, feelings, and actions. Only in fairy tales can a wizard cast a magic spell to make people's own minds play tricks on them. In real life, we know that no one causes mental illness. It is no one's fault that your parent has mental illness.

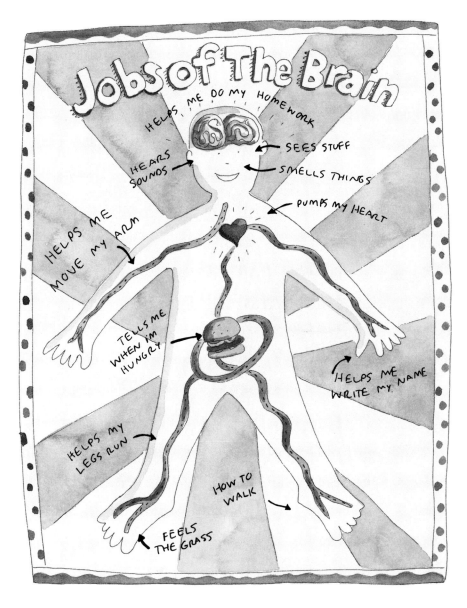

Jobs of The Brain

HELPS ME DO MY HOMEWORK

SEES STUFF

SMELLS THINGS

HEARS SOUNDS

PUMPS MY HEART

HELPS ME MOVE MY ARM

TELLS ME WHEN I'M HUNGRY

HELPS ME WRITE MY NAME

HELPS MY LEGS RUN

HOW TO WALK

FEELS THE GRASS

Your brain is the control center of everything you do. It has many, many jobs to do to keep you and your body working. The brain is very complex and more powerful than any computer ever made.

The brain is helped by nerves all over your body that lead back to the brain, like roads leading into a big, busy city. The nerves in your body send millions of signals to your brain every day. These signals carry messages about what you see, hear, smell, taste, and touch. Your brain then decides what to do about each message—what to feel, how to act, what to say, and what to remember.

Different kinds of chemicals help carry the signals and messages in and out of the brain. These chemicals have to be in the right balance for the brain to work right. When the chemicals are not balanced, it's hard for the brain to figure out the incoming signals and to sort out all the messages.

When that happens, normal brain activities like thinking and imagining don't work the way they are supposed to. This can cause the person with a mental illness to feel extreme amounts of an emotion like fear or sadness, or not be able to tell if something is real or imaginary.

Doctors and scientists don't always know exactly what causes the chemicals to be out of balance. But they do believe that when a person has a mental illness, this is what has happened with the chemicals that make the brain work.

Your A-maze-ing Brain

Your brain is made up of billions of tiny cells, all connected together in millions of pathways. In fact, your brain has so many pathways that if you strung them out in a line, they could stretch to the moon and back! The way they are arranged inside your brain is more complicated than the toughest maze ever built. Many scientists spend their whole lives trying to map out a small part of the brain and its pathways to learn more about how each part works and connects with all the other parts.

See if you can find a way through the Brain Maze. As hard as it might be, your own brain's pathways are much more complicated and "a-maze-ing"!

BRAIN MAZE

START HERE

FINISH HERE

Stress and Mental Illness

Many doctors and scientists think that serious stress can help cause mental illness or make it worse. When we talk about stress, we are usually talking about the worries and tension that live inside all of us and that sometimes make it hard to relax and enjoy life.

Stress can also make people feel extra sad, tired, confused, or angry. Serious stress means very big adult problems that seem to go on and on, making people feel worn out and helpless.

When people don't know how to handle serious stress, their problems can get even bigger. Sometimes when people are having problems or feeling bad, they don't know how to talk about these things in ways that are helpful or healthy.

Instead, they keep their feelings inside, or they deal with them in unhealthy ways—ways that can cause even more problems. This can contribute to mental illness too.

Can you think of some healthy ways to deal with worries and problems?

Have you noticed your parent trying to deal with stress in ways that are unhealthy or that don't work? What are they?

Symptoms of Mental Illness

Different mental illnesses cause people to think, feel, and act in different ways. All of these different ways are known as the signs or symptoms of the illness.

As you already know, mental illness makes it hard for your mom or dad to think clearly. Some thinking problems that mental illness can cause include:

- ☐ not being able to concentrate or focus the mind
- ☐ forgetting things, such as your birthday
- ☐ not being able to think through little problems they could normally handle
- ☐ imagining things are happening when they really aren't
- ☐ imagining voices or sounds that aren't really there
- ☐ imagining people are doing things, such as spying, when they really aren't
- ☐ imagining they can do anything, as if they are a superhero
- ☐ believing they deserve special treatment, like a queen or king

When people have trouble thinking clearly, they often do things that don't make sense to you or others. People with mental illness may do any of these kinds of things:

- ☐ talk a lot to themselves
- ☐ talk to others who aren't real (imaginary people)
- ☐ talk to others who aren't really there at the moment
- ☐ talk without stopping, jumping from topic to topic
- ☐ mumble or use words that don't make sense to others
- ☐ repeat the same sentences over and over
- ☐ whisper, yell, scream, laugh, or cry without a reason you can understand
- ☐ laugh at a sad story or cry at a funny story
- ☐ refuse to talk or answer anyone's questions, when usually they would talk and answer
- ☐ hide from others
- ☐ not trust someone they usually would trust
- ☐ refuse to go outside or move around much
- ☐ sleep all the time or stay in bed
- ☐ stay awake all the time with no sleep at all
- ☐ move or exercise constantly

- ☐ go back and forth from being very active to not active at all
- ☐ repeat things like pacing the floor or checking to see if someone is at the door over and over
- ☐ refuse to let you or others do things they usually wouldn't care about
- ☐ stare or glare at you or others
- ☐ demand that others do things they usually wouldn't ask anyone to do
- ☐ accuse others of doing things they didn't do
- ☐ show no interest in things they normally would be interested in
- ☐ refuse to touch things or others
- ☐ get angry when touched by others
- ☐ be impatient and get unexpectedly angry with others
- ☐ refuse to get dressed or change clothes
- ☐ refuse to bathe or shower
- ☐ refuse to eat properly

Mental illness can also make a person be unable to show any emotions at all. On the other hand, it can make someone feel any of these emotions more than usual:

- ☐ scared, afraid, worried, anxious
- ☐ untrusting, suspicious, paranoid
- ☐ sad, depressed, hopeless
- ☐ mad, angry, upset

- ☐ frustrated, agitated, disturbed
- ☐ giggly, excited, hyper, manic, super-energetic
- ☐ lonely, isolated, alienated
- ☐ powerless, helpless

SCARED   UPSET   GIGGLY   HOPELESS

Look again at these lists of symptoms. Put a check mark next to each one you think your parent has thought, done, or felt.

As you know, it's not fun to be ill. That's especially true with a mental illness. Mental illness can cause a lot of problems for parents and make them feel bad. For kids, it hurts a lot to see their mom or dad suffer.

It is really important for kids to remember that they are not to blame for their parent's mental illness. It's also important for you to know that your mom or dad can get help.

A Chain of Symptoms

When people have a mental illness, they can sometimes tell when they are getting ill again. Sometimes their kids can tell too. They may see a pattern of behavior, or a "chain of symptoms," that tells them their parent is having what's called a relapse. *Relapse* means someone is ill again after a period of being better or being well.

This can be really helpful for you to know. If you see signs that make you think your mom or dad might be getting ill again, you can tell your parent or someone else so he or she can get help more quickly.

Since each person's symptoms are unique, usually only a family member or close friend will notice early signs. But even they might not notice, because some people don't show any signs at all. Don't feel bad if you don't notice anything different. Your parent might not show in any way that a relapse is coming.

The symptoms that are most often noticed are:

- ☐ not sleeping, or sleeping poorly, for several nights in a row
- ☐ a general lack of interest in things
- ☐ not doing things they usually do
- ☐ paying less attention to being clean and how they look
- ☐ mood swings
- ☐ signs that their mind is playing tricks on them

If you think you may have noticed some symptoms, complete the following sentences.

What I first notice when my parent has started to get ill is:

What I notice next is:

If I think they are getting ill again, I will tell:

_____.

Treatment of Mental Illness

The symptoms of mental illness are treated best with a combination of two important things: medication and psychotherapy.

MEDICATION

Medications (another word for medicines) can help balance the chemicals in the brain to make it work better. This reduces some mixed-up thoughts and behaviors that are the symptoms of mental illness. While doctors can't see exactly what signals are getting mixed up, they try to figure out which chemicals the brain needs to get in balance. These chemicals are in the medicines that doctors give to their patients with mental illnesses to help them get better.

Sometimes people don't like to take medication. They may think it doesn't work. Medicine does different things to different people, because no two people's brains are exactly the same. Because of this, doctors may need to try several kinds of medications before they find the ones that do the best job of helping a person's symptoms of mental illness. Also, it often takes a few weeks for some pills to start working well. It's important that people stick with it long enough to find the right medicine and for it to start working.

Another problem with medications is that they may cause side effects that people don't like. This means that even though the pills help stop the symptoms, the pills might also make a person feel something else that's uncomfortable, such as tired, restless, thirsty, or hungry all the time. Doctors can often help make these side effects less bothersome by fixing the amount of medicine a person takes, or by trying a different medicine.

PSYCHOTHERAPY

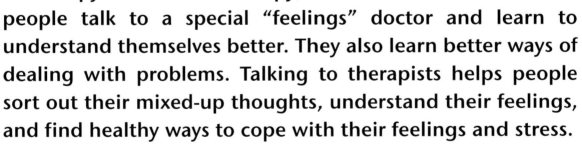

The other part of treatment that helps people with mental illness is psychotherapy, or therapy for short. In therapy, people talk to a special "feelings" doctor and learn to understand themselves better. They also learn better ways of dealing with problems. Talking to therapists helps people sort out their mixed-up thoughts, understand their feelings, and find healthy ways to cope with their feelings and stress.

It may seem like a long time before your parent feels better and back to normal. As this happens, some people may consider your parent cured. You might even feel this way too. Your parent can get better with the right treatment and be able to function in a normal day-to-day way for a very long time. You need to know, though, that your parent's illness may not disappear forever. It may come back from time to time.

A Dictionary of Words About Mental Illness

There are lots of special words to describe mental illness, its symptoms, and its treatment. There are even special names for some kinds of helpers. You have probably heard your parent or other adults use some of these words. See how many new words you can learn. Ask your therapist or another trusted adult to pronounce the ones you don't know.

The words in this dictionary are in alphabetical order. When a definition has a word in extra dark type, that dark word can also be found as an entry in this dictionary.

DICTIONARY

Anxiety, anxious. Feelings of fear and jumpiness, sometimes without a reason.

Anxiety attack. Sudden, extreme fears that make a person think something very bad is going to happen. Usually the fears are so strong that people have symptoms in their bodies too, such as breathing trouble or a heart beating too fast. They may think they are having a heart attack or even fear they are going to die.

Bipolar affective disorder, bipolar disorder. A mental illness characterized by extremes in mood and energy level, as well as **delusions**. A person with this disorder may feel very excited and energetic one day, and then very tired and hopeless the next.

Compulsion. An action, such as checking a locked door or washing hands, that someone feels they must do over and over. People usually think something bad will happen if they stop doing this action. Compulsions are often the result of a certain kind of thought called an **obsession.**

Confusion. Not being sure you understand something, or having mixed-up thoughts or feelings.

Counselor. A helper who provides support with sorting out feelings, setting goals, and making choices to help people solve their own problems.

Delusion. A symptom of mental illness having to do with a person's ability to think. A delusion is a thought a person believes is true, even when the person is given evidence that it is false.

Depression. A mental illness characterized by feelings of sadness, worthlessness, hopelessness, and lack of energy for long periods of time. People with depression feel unhappy for no reason or about little things that usually didn't make them feel very sad before. When people are depressed, they often aren't interested in anything, even things they used to enjoy. They don't want to feel this way, but they can't help it.

Disorder. A serious health problem or illness.

Hallucination. A symptom of mental illness having to do with the senses. A person has a hallucination when he or she sees, hears, smells, tastes, or feels things that aren't really there.

Manic depression. Another term for **bipolar affective disorder;** it isn't used often anymore.

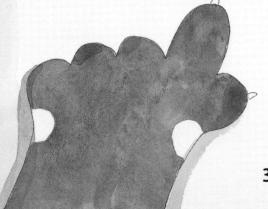

36

Mania, manic episode. When someone with mental illness has an extremely energetic feeling such as excitement that lasts much longer than normal, such as several days. During manic episodes, people often have so many thoughts and ideas they can hardly keep up with them, and they speak very fast. They may have so much energy they can't sleep. And they think they are able to do just about anything. They are usually too distracted to finish much, though, and may feel very irritable.

Obsession. A type of thought pattern that a person has difficulty controlling. A person with an obsession keeps thinking the same unwanted thought over and over. To try to stop an obsession, people often respond with a **compulsion**.

Panic attack. Another term for **anxiety attack**.

Paranoia. A symptom of mental illness. With paranoia, people believe that others are trying to cause harm; they are usually very suspicious and do not trust others.

Phobias. Very big, unreasonable fears of things that are not frightening to most people. Phobias can make people avoid doing certain things, even though they want to be able to do them. For example, a person may have a phobia of going outside or being around water.

Psychiatrist. A type of medical doctor whose specialty is treatment of mental illness and diseases of the brain. A psychiatrist can decide what medication a person with mental illness needs, and suggest other forms of treatment.

Psychologist. A type of scientist or doctor whose specialty is understanding how people think, feel, and behave. When treating people who have a mental illness, a psychologist works as a **psychotherapist**, helping a person understand his or her thoughts and feelings, learn to solve problems and cope with stressful events, and find healthy ways to behave and express feelings.

Psychosis, psychotic. Any mental illness that involves not knowing what is real and what is imaginary.

Psychotherapy, therapy. A form of treatment that involves talking with people to help them sort out their thoughts and feelings, and learn healthy ways of dealing with problems and making choices. It also helps with such things as handling stress, improving communication with people, and feeling better overall.

Psychotherapist, therapist. A person who specializes in psychotherapy. There are many kinds of therapists, including psychologists, psychiatrists, clinical social workers, and psychiatric nurses. Each kind of therapist has attended a special type of school for a long time and has a special focus in helping people improve their health and well-being.

Schizophrenia. A **psychotic** disorder. People with schizophrenia usually have **delusions** and **hallucinations**. Their behavior and personality change as the disease gets worse, and they are not able to lead normal lives because they often can't tell what is real.

Stress. Worries, tension, and problems that make it hard for people to relax and enjoy life. Stress can affect our bodies by making us feel tired or achy. The most serious kind of stress can contribute to illness, including mental illness.

Symptoms. Signs of illness. **Delusions**, long periods of sadness, and **compulsions** are a few symptoms of mental illness.

Treatment. Things that medical doctors, therapists, and other helpers do to help people with mental illness get better. These include prescribing medications and providing psychotherapy.

Are there other words you have heard but don't know their meaning? Ask someone such as your parent or therapist what they mean.

Other Facts About Mental Illness

Men and women from every country, culture, race, and religion around the world can suffer from a mental illness. In fact, about one out of every five people will have some form of mental illness during their life.

Most kinds of mental illness do not cause people to see or hear things that aren't real, and don't make it too hard for a person to have friends, families, and jobs. Most people who get a mental illness will suffer from a kind that can be treated with medication and psychotherapy. These milder kinds often involve feelings of depression or anxiety that last longer and are stronger than the normal feelings of sadness and worry that all people usually feel.

Mental illnesses such as schizophrenia and bipolar affective disorder are more rare. They are tougher to treat and to cope with, and their symptoms are usually more noticeable to others. These are sometimes referred to as "major mental illnesses," because they involve a chemical imbalance in parts of the brain that control thinking and use of the imagination. This causes more mixed-up thinking and difficulties knowing what is real or imaginary.

Parents who suffer from one of these major diseases will always have their mental illness, but with the right treatments and support, the symptoms can be made smaller, and parents can be like parents again.

Doctors and scientists from all over the world are working hard to find better medications and trying to find a cure for all mental illnesses.

CHAPTER 3

YOUR FEELINGS AND WHAT TO DO WITH THEM

Everyone feels all kinds of feelings. You know what it's like to feel happy, lonely, sad, angry, embarrassed, loving, proud, afraid, and calm.

In this chapter we are going to talk about what kinds of feelings most kids say they've had when their parent has a mental illness. We will also explore healthy ways to show your feelings and healthy ways to relax and feel better. Understanding your feelings and letting go of your worries is very important for your happiness and well-being.

All Feelings Are Okay

Most kids sometimes feel confused or scared when a parent has a mental illness. They aren't sure how their parent is going to act, and sometimes they don't know what to do themselves. Kids can easily end up feeling stressed and helpless.

Some kids feel angry, ashamed, or embarrassed when their parent's illness makes him or her act in an unusual way. You might not want others to know that your parent has a mental illness and acts in ways that others might think are strange. Even though you know your parent can't help it that he or she is ill, you still feel this way.

When kids have a parent with mental illness, these feelings are all NORMAL! The important thing is for you to understand your feelings and to figure out how to deal with whatever comes your way.

How do you feel right now?

When my parent is acting unusual, I feel:

My brothers and sisters say they feel:

When my parent is very ill, I want to:

What I usually do is:

FEELING WORD CLUSTERS

Fill in all the words you know that have a similar meaning to each of the four feeling words below.

Lots of times you can tell how people are feeling just by the look on their face. Can you give a feeling word to each face below?

_____ _____ _____

Now draw your own cartoon faces to show feelings you've had, and write the feeling words underneath them.

_____ _____ _____

Talking About Your Feelings

Remember that it's okay to feel whatever you feel, and that your feelings are normal. Sharing feelings with another person may help you feel better when you're sad or angry or scared. Talking with someone almost always helps us feel less lonely.

Most young people say it helps to talk with a grown-up, such as a grandparent or a teacher or a therapist. Some also like to talk to a trusted friend their own age, or to a brother or sister.

The people who have helped me most to talk about my feelings are:

Their phone numbers are:

The most helpful things they said were:

Hidden Feelings

Some kids find it hard to talk about their feelings. They are used to keeping lots of feelings inside, and they hide their feelings for all kinds of reasons.

Some kids think their feelings aren't important to other people. Some worry that they'll get into trouble for having the feelings. And many think they may hurt someone by saying what they really feel.

But all of your feelings are important, and talking about them is okay. Maybe you have some feelings you keep hidden or feel shy about sharing. It may be helpful to think about those hidden feelings as something like buried treasure.

If you feel comfortable, write those hidden feelings
on the buried treasure map above.

A FEELINGS TREASURE CHEST

You can make a treasure chest for your feelings. You'll need scissors, glue, and markers or crayons for decorating your treasure chest.

DIRECTIONS:

1 Using your scissors, cut carefully along the solid lines of the Treasure Chest Design on the next page. Do not cut along the dotted lines.

2 Turn the paper over to the blank side and decorate it. This is the outside of your Treasure Chest. Next, fold the paper inward along the dotted lines.

3 Glue the sides of the lid together first, then the sides of the Chest, followed by the remaining flap folds. Your finished Treasure Chest should look like this: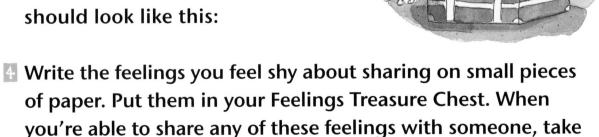

4 Write the feelings you feel shy about sharing on small pieces of paper. Put them in your Feelings Treasure Chest. When you're able to share any of these feelings with someone, take them out of the Chest.

TREASURE CHEST DESIGN

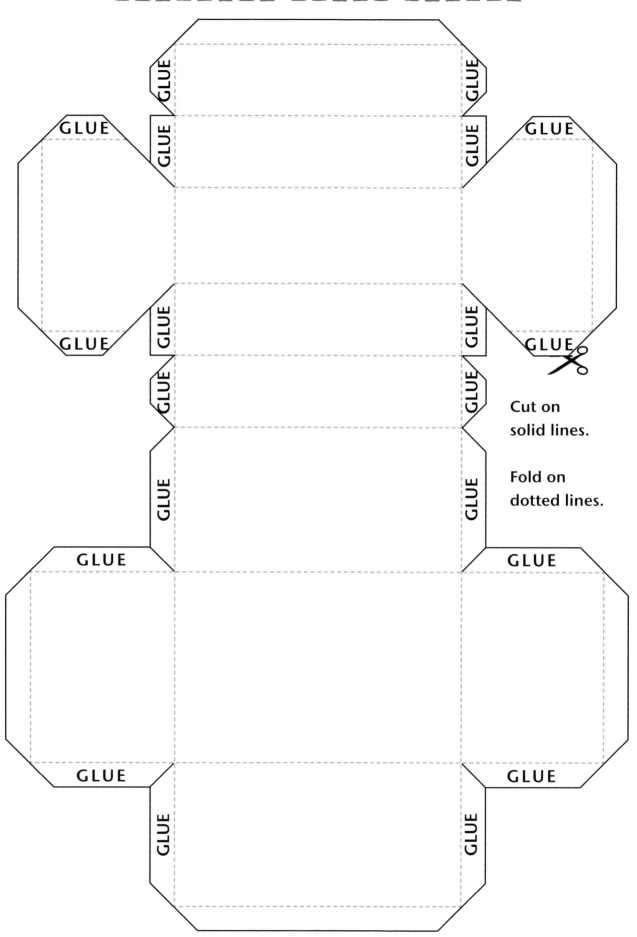

Cut on
solid lines.

Fold on
dotted lines.

What would help you open your treasure chest and share more of your feelings?

Which of these feelings would be easiest to share?

Feelings are as precious as ...

Feeling Safe

Sometimes kids feel scared by things their mom or dad says or does when ill. Your parent may imagine scary things, or imagine that something or someone is trying to hurt him or her, or you, or others in your family. Or your parent might think about a situation in a strange or unusual way, and thinking of it that way might make him or her feel nervous or scared.

This sometimes happens to people with mental illness. They can't always know what's real and what's imaginary. This can cause your parent to have trouble trusting people, make it hard for him or her to believe that things are fine, or make him or her act in a strange way. Your parent probably just wants to protect you from someone or something that seems like a threat to your safety, because he or she loves you.

People with mental illness don't mean to say or do things that bother others. They might not even believe it when someone tells them they have imagined something. They still think it's real. But if things get too scary for you, or if you feel uncomfortable or unsafe, it's important for you to tell a grown-up. All kids need to feel safe!

I feel uncomfortable or scared when:

If this happens again, I will tell_____.

I will also do these things to feel safe:

Feelings Over Time

If you're like most kids, your feelings about lots of things have changed over time. When you first found out about your parent's illness, maybe you felt shocked and confused. But now you might feel relieved to know what is causing your parent to act in ways you don't understand.

Most kids feel angry at times because it seems so unfair that their parent has a mental illness. You might also feel worried and sad for your mom or dad. And even though you know your parent isn't ill on purpose, sometimes you might feel upset, uncomfortable, hurt, or embarrassed by some of the things he or she says and does.

When I think about my parent's illness, here are some of the feelings I have had:

Finding Healthy Ways to Show Feelings

Uncomfortable feelings usually go away faster if you express them in a healthy way when you feel them. A healthy way is a way that helps problems get smaller or go away. Unhealthy ways are ways that make the problem worse or cause other problems.

Most kids say it doesn't help to pretend that they are okay when they're really feeling sad, worried, or upset. You also don't have to act tough or try to put on a brave front. When you hold in your upset feelings, you usually just get more upset. If you get angry, you might take it out on someone else by being unkind. If you do that, you will probably feel bad, or you'll get into trouble and then feel even worse!

Talk with your therapist, school counselor, or another adult you trust about some healthy ways to let your feelings out.

It's important for all people (both kids and grown-ups) to find healthy ways to show their feelings. Therapists, counselors, and other adults can help you learn many good ways. What are some of the ways you have learned?

When I feel happy, I can show it by:

When I feel sad, I can show it by:

When I feel angry, I can show it by:

When I feel lonely, I can show it by:

**When I feel scared,
I can show it by:**

When I feel_____, I can show it by:

Letting Go of Worries

Many kids who have a parent with mental illness worry about all sorts of things.

You might worry about your schoolwork or grades because you have trouble concentrating at school.

You might worry about what other people think of your mom or dad.

You might worry so much that you have trouble falling asleep at night or you have nightmares.

You might even be worried that you will get a mental illness yourself. You should know right now that you aren't likely to get a mental illness. And the chances that you'll have a mental illness are even less if you learn healthy ways to express your feelings and to handle the stress in your life.

Reading this book and talking about your feelings are two important things you can do to help some of your worries go away. Learning more about mental illness and your parent will help too.

Whatever it is you worry about, you can talk to a grown-up you trust about it.

I have worried or wondered about:

I talked to_____about my worries.

What_____said that helped me
let go of my worries was:

If I have questions or things that worry me,
I will talk to:_____,
or to_____,
or to_____.

Having Fun and Feeling Like You

Some kids say they find it hard to enjoy being a normal kid and to have fun. Things like clowning around and being silly and playful are harder when you worry a lot or when you see a parent feeling sad or worried.

Do you think there is such a thing as being too silly? If you find yourself thinking badly of other kids when they are playful, chances are you aren't having enough fun yourself.

Some kids say it helps to read cartoons or funny stories and jokes every morning. Some kids like to think of fun things they have done or fun ways to play.

If you are serious a lot of the time, create a list of fun things to do, keep adding to it, and go ahead and have some fun!

FUN THINGS TO DO

1. _____

2. _____

3. _____

4. _____

5. _____

6. _____

7. _____

8. _____

9. _____

10. _____

11. _____

12. _____

13. _____

Learning to Relax

Having a parent who is mentally ill can be very stressful. Often when we're stressed, we tighten up our muscles and keep them tense for long periods of time. People hold stress in their shoulders or their stomach or their face. One way to relieve stress is to relax those parts of your body that are tense.

Learning how to relax and let your stress go can help you have more fun. To find where you hold stress in your body, ask yourself, "When I am angry or sad or scared, where do I feel it in my body?" Or pretend you're having a stress-making feeling right now to figure out which muscles you tense. Once you have found your stress spots, you can create a Stress Map.

DIRECTIONS:

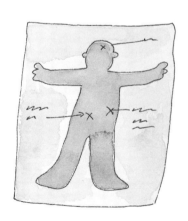

1 Look at the body on the next page.

2 Write feeling words on the places where you feel stress. Use words like MAD, SAD, SCARED, WORRIED, and UPSET. You can also use just STRESSED.

3 When you're feeling stressed, relax the areas of your body that you marked on your Stress Map. You'll feel better!

STRESS MAP

DEEP BREATHING EXERCISE

Relaxing deeply is a great way to get rid of stress and keep it from building back up. If you practice relaxing every day, you'll find that it's easier to relax when stressful things happen. Try this exercise every day for the next week.

DIRECTIONS:

1 Lie on a couch or a soft rug or padded mat on the floor.

2 Take in a long, deep breath through your nose while you count slowly to 5.

3 Hold it while counting to 5 again.

4 Slowly exhale the breath.

5 Repeat this for a couple minutes.

6 Next, you are going to tighten up the muscles in different parts of your body while you continue to do the deep breathing. You'll start with the muscles in the lowest part of the body and move up, tightening the muscles in different parts of your body with each breath. Start with the feet.

7 As you breathe in, tighten the muscles in your feet. Squeeze hard! Hold the squeeze in your feet while you count to 5.

8 When you breathe out, let your feet go totally limp. Take another deep in-and-out breath without tightening any muscles up.

9 Now repeat this with the different muscle groups in the rest of your body. After your feet, do your legs, back, stomach, hands, arms, shoulders, and last, your face.

Do you feel relaxed now? The next time you do this exercise, you can play some soft, soothing music in the background. You might also try thinking of a peaceful place, such as a beach, and imagining yourself there.

TURNING YOUR TROUBLES INTO BUBBLES

If you have a bubble ring and some bubble soap, you might want to try this activity when you are worrying a lot. It's simple, but it works!

Just go outside and blow some bubbles. With each bubble you blow, think of one of the worries you have, and say this poem to yourself:

I'm turning my troubles
Into harmless bubbles,
Letting the wind set them free,
Lifting all my worries from me.

Some bubbles disappear so fast,
It's only for a moment they last,
While others seem to float all day,
Taking my troubles far away.

There are many other things you can do to relieve stress and worry. Some kids like to write out their worries on bits of paper and then float them down a stream. You could even tape them to a helium balloon and watch them float away. You might try writing your troubles inside these bubbles on this page.

Feeling Guilty

Sometimes kids think they made their mom or dad get a mental illness by doing something wrong or by not doing what they were told to do. Maybe you didn't do your chores, or you got bad grades in school, or you argued with your parent. All kids get frustrated with their mom, dad, family, and others some of the time. Of course, your parent probably doesn't enjoy it when these things happen, but none of these things can cause someone to have a mental illness.

Draw something that made you feel guilty.

If you ever thought or wondered if you were to blame for your parent's illness, you may have felt guilty. There is no need to feel this way. You are not to blame. Even if someone tries to tell you differently, remember:

KIDS DON'T CAUSE MENTAL ILLNESS!

Also, remember this:

MY PLAN

The next time I feel stressed or worried I will:

CHAPTER 4

OTHER PEOPLE'S FEARS OF MENTAL ILLNESS

Y ou probably know other people who don't know very much about mental illness. Some of them may have false information about it and not know where to get the truth. It can be hard to talk to people who have a lot of false ideas about mental illness. In this chapter you will learn more about how you could try to help educate others about mental illness.

You will also learn healthy ways to be yourself and help your parent out. We'll discuss stressful situations, such as dealing with other people's fears and questions. We will also talk about being respectful of differences, for as you know, no two people are exactly the same. And finally, you'll learn new ways you can express yourself and feel proud of being your own unique person.

Dealing with Name Calling

Most people know very little about mental illness, and some feel nervous, shy, or scared around others who are acting in unusual ways. Some people even make fun of those who act differently. They may call people with mental illness hurtful names like "crazy" or "weird."

Name calling can really hurt! You may have heard someone make fun of your parent. You may even have felt angry, hurt, or ashamed because of the mean things people have said. You know your parent can't always stop or change the way he or she is acting, thinking, or feeling. As you know, no one wants or chooses to have a mental illness. Making fun of people who can't change their illness is unkind and unfeeling.

Some people misunderstand or are afraid of anyone who is different than they are. For example, many people are afraid that people with mental illness are dangerous or violent. This is untrue. People with mental illness are actually more likely to be timid and afraid of being hurt by others.

When people feel scared, that fear sometimes turns into disrespect and meanness. We call that prejudice. People act on their prejudices by ignoring, bullying, or teasing others. People who are ill or disabled are often the target of prejudice. They may feel hurt and ashamed of their differences, even though they can't change the way they are different. Everyone wants to be accepted and appreciated by other people. Everyone wants to belong with other people.

What do you think the world would be like if there were no differences and we all were exactly alike?

Celebrating How We Are Different and Alike

All people are alike in some ways and different in others. Even twins are not exactly the same. We all have different likes, experiences, histories, dreams, abilities, skills, talents, wants, looks, values, beliefs, thoughts, feelings, and more!

One thing that makes me different from my best friend is:

Some ways I am different from my brother or sister are:

Some ways I am different from my parents are:

Some ways I am different from my
classmates are:

Some ways I am like my
best friend are:

Some ways I am like my brother or sister are:

Some ways I am like my parents are:

I'M UNIQUE

*Cut and paste some pictures of people who look
different from you and each other in the space above.
Old magazines are a good place to find interesting faces.*

Standing Up
Against Prejudice

If you have ever been the target of prejudice, you probably felt lonely and scared. When people are being picked on, they need others to stick up for them and their right to be treated well. Everyone deserves to be treated fairly. Standing together against prejudice, bullying, and unfriendly teasing usually stops these actions.

It can be scary to stick up for yourself or someone else. People who are being mean don't like to have their behavior pointed out by others. They might even try to tease or bully anyone who says they are being unfair to someone. (Bullies do this to try to make you feel bad about yourself so you'll be quiet and stop accusing them.)

Most people try to ignore anyone who makes cruel comments or acts like a bully. Sometimes this is the best or easiest way to deal with a bully. Other times, it is important to tell others how you feel about what they say or do. Sometimes people don't realize their actions are hurtful until you tell them. Once they know this, they can choose to act differently next time.

Everyone deserves to be treated with respect and kindness. Being nice to others makes all of our lives better.

Protecting Yourself from Bullying

Long ago, people put what's called a coat of arms or a family crest on protective shields. They often displayed words like TRUTH, JUSTICE, and COURAGE on their shields to inspire themselves. They also put pictures on their shields that made them feel proud and reminded them of their family and history.

You can make and decorate your own protective shield with words and images to help you feel better if you've ever felt bullied. Try writing a motto on it, too, such as:

I celebrate different-ness.
I am powerful and brave.
I stick up for myself.
I ignore cruel comments.
I can protect myself from hurtful words.
I am unique, and I belong here.
I am strong, courageous, and kind.
I have good things in common with others.

What other kinds of things could you say to inspire yourself and ignore hurtful comments?

Using "I" Statements

When people are upset, they sometimes blame others, and sometimes use an angry, loud voice. This may make others feel attacked. When people feel attacked, they usually stop listening to whatever is being said. No one likes to be spoken to this way.

If we express our thoughts, wants, and feelings in such a way that we aren't blaming other people, then our words are easier for others to hear. Using statements that start with "I" often helps others listen to us. Here are some examples:

See if you can write some of your own "I" statements. You may want to ask someone else, such as your therapist, to help you write and then practice using them. Try to speak calmly and look straight into the eyes of the person you're talking to. Standing up for yourself like this is called being assertive!

I feel_____

when you_____.

I think_____

when you_____.

I want_____

when you_____.

I am going to_____

when you_____.

In the future, I will_____

when you_____.

Learning to Assert Yourself with Practice

Sometimes it's hard to speak up, especially when you feel stressed or are afraid. Practice can make it easier to be assertive. To practice, try a role-play or rehearsal with someone such as your therapist.

First, let your therapist or partner play the assertive role, while you play the person who makes a mean comment. Then switch roles. Just play act and make it up as you go along. When you are playing the bully role, try to say things you think someone who is prejudiced would say.

Don't get discouraged if you find it hard to be assertive at first. Ask your partner to coach you, then write a list of what assertive "I" statements you'd like to say.

In the future, I want to say:

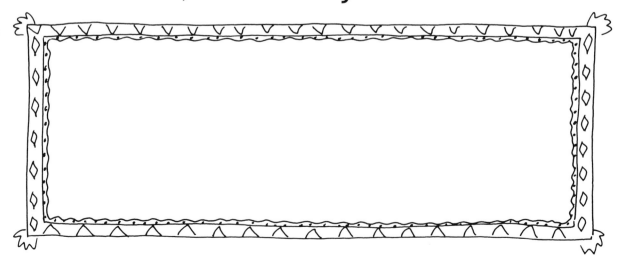

Telling Others About Your Parent

Do you find it hard to know what to say when people ask about your parent? Most people ask because they care about you and your mom or dad. They also might be interested in helping out if they can. Others, though, may be curious about what's "wrong" with them. It's important that you say only what makes you comfortable.

Some parents and their kids tell others that they have a physical illness. (The brain is part of the body, after all.) Others like to use terms like chemical imbalance, psychiatric disability, or mental illness. This can be an opportunity for you to educate your friends or other people about the facts of mental illness.

You and your family might not want to say anything, or you might tell people that it is personal or a private family matter. What you tell other people is totally up to you and your family. It might be helpful to discuss this with your family and others you trust, such as your therapist, and hear their ideas. This will help you be better prepared to answer these kinds of questions.

What I am comfortable telling others who ask about my parent's illness is:

CHAPTER 5

YOUR PLACE IN THE FAMILY

You are a very important part of your family. You do chores, and you might watch after your brother or sister from time to time. You probably help your parents out with other things when they ask. But sometimes this may feel like too much to handle on your own. And maybe it is. In this chapter, you will learn what kid-size responsibilities are, and what's too much. And you'll learn that when a parent isn't able to do everything needed for the family and the home, it's time for other adults to help.

Family Rules

All families have different rules about who does what to help take care of the home and everyone in it. When a family has an ill parent, extra adult help may be needed with some of the chores. Also, each family member may need to do a little more than usual. This is the case whether a parent has a mental illness or an illness in their body.

Kids often feel ashamed that their parent has a mental illness, and they want to keep it a secret. To try to keep their homes looking "normal," they end up doing all the household chores. They may try to do all the laundry, cooking, and cleaning, as well as looking after their younger brothers and sisters. No child should try to do all the work alone. Some jobs are just too hard for a kid, and some are the responsibilities of grown-ups. Grown-up responsibilities are things like cooking, grocery shopping, and most big cleaning and laundry chores.

When your parent can't do all the things that grown-ups are responsible for, other adults need to fill in, not you. Kids need to do kid-size chores, like making their bed, feeding their pets, and keeping their room tidy.

As a kid, you need lots of time for playing, going to school, doing homework, and even doing nothing at all, except maybe daydreaming and relaxing. Kids also need time for hobbies and other things that interest them and make them feel good, like talking to a friend or cuddling the family pet.

MY FAVORITE FUN THING

Draw a picture of your favorite fun thing.

Kid-size Chores

Some parents find it hard to let their children do things on their own and become more independent. Other parents sometimes find it hard to remember that their kids are only kids and shouldn't do more grown-up chores until they are older. Sometimes parents forget that another friend or family member can pitch in and help do big chores when they are tired or don't feel up to it. If you need help with your chores or your parent needs help with grown-up chores, ask an adult to help you.

Fun things I can do on my own are:

Fun things I still like or need help with are:

Chores I often do are:

**Chores I do every
once in a while are:**

Chores I can't do well on my own yet are:

Chores I really hate doing are:

Chores I am really good at doing are:

Who Looks After You

Being a parent is a very big and important job! At times, parents with mental illness can't look after their own children. (This usually makes them feel extra sad.) When they can't look after their children, other adults need to do it for them.

Some kids stay with grandparents, aunts, uncles, family friends, or foster parents. These grown-ups can help kids feel loved and safe when their parent can't be with them.

If my parent is too ill to look after me, I will

stay with_____, or I will

be looked after by_____

in my own home.

Visits with Your Parent

Sometimes when people with mental illness need extra help taking care of themselves, they go to stay in a hospital, mental health clinic, or treatment center. Maybe your parent has stayed at a place like this before, or is just starting to live there now.

When people with mental illness stay at a treatment center, they get lots of rest and help from doctors, psychologists, therapists, and nurses. A whole team of people will work to figure out how to best treat your parent. Your parent will probably receive medications. And he or she will probably talk about problems and feelings in sessions with a psychologist or other therapist.

Some kids have weekly visits with their parents when they don't live with them or when their parents are in a treatment center. Most kids look forward to spending happy times with their mom or dad when the parent is feeling well. Sometimes, though, another grown-up goes along to be sure a child feels safe and has a good time. This often happens when a parent is having symptoms or is not feeling well.

Some parents don't like having another grown-up around during their visits with their children. They might imagine they're being watched all the time, and they don't like it. Some parents worry that other grown-ups will turn their child against them and can't be trusted.

People with mental illness often feel scared and powerless when they are unable to control things in their mind or things around them. If this happens to your parent, remember that your parent wants to see you and loves you. If your parent is upset or not wanting to talk or play with you on a visit, or is unable to make one of your visits at all, you may feel bad. Try to remember that you're not to blame. It's your parent's illness—not you—that is making him or her feel this way!

What You Can Do to Help Out

If you notice your parent behaving in ways that make you think he or she is getting ill, you can help.

Ways to be helpful:
✔ tell another adult, who can encourage your parent to get help as soon as possible
✔ avoid arguing with your parent
✔ talk to your parent quietly, speak slowly, and use short sentences
✔ try to remain calm and use your stress management and relaxation skills
✔ call a trusted adult or your own therapist for help

Also, it's important that you:
✔ ask your therapist or trusted adult for help whenever you need it
✔ try to keep up your schoolwork, routines, and outside interests
✔ be good to yourself and let yourself be a kid
✔ stay connected to your friends and other family
✔ remember it's not your fault that your parent is ill

Other ways I know I can be helpful:
✔ _____
✔ _____

Learning Summary

Wow! There is so much to learn and to know about mental illness. You probably already knew some things about it before you started reading this book. This might be a good time to think about what you know after reading the book this far.

New things I've learned about my parent's mental illness are:

Things I really want to remember are:

Other things I still want to know about my parent's illness are:

I will ask _____ about these things.

CHAPTER 6

BUILDING ON YOUR STRENGTHS AND SUPPORTS

There are so many ways you can be good to yourself. In this chapter we'll discuss lots of them. You may even learn some new things about yourself, things about you that make you feel proud of yourself! Thinking positively and sharing with others can really help you feel better. We'll also talk about your dreams for the future and any advice you might have for other kids.

MY FAVORITE MEMORIES

Remembering happy times with your parent can help you feel better when you feel sad or worried. It can help you feel stronger and braver too.

List your favorite memories of times you have spent with your parent so that you can read them the next time you feel sad.

1 _____

2 _____

3 _____

4 _____

5 _____

6 _____

7 _____

8 _____

9 _____

10 _____

Draw a picture of your favorite time, or write about this memory for your parent. Your parent can look at it if he or she is feeling sad or lonely.

If you have been able to share some of your feelings you once kept hidden in your Feelings Treasure Chest, you might now have room to store happy memories in it!

The next time you're having a good time with your mom or dad, tell him or her.

Being Happy

All kids have the right to be happy. When your parent is ill, you may want to cheer yourself up and take your mind off your parent's illness or your own struggles.

Write a list of things you like to do and ways you can be good to yourself. The next time you are feeling unhappy, do something on this list.

1 _____

2 _____

3 _____

4 _____

5 _____

6 _____

7 _____

8 _____

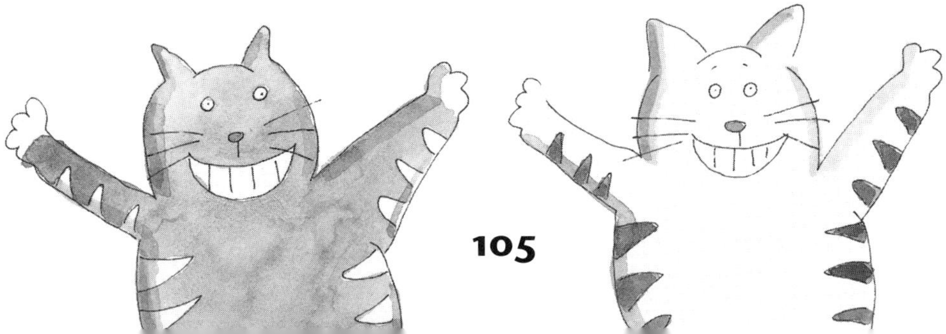

"Feeling Good" Activities

Some kids say they find it hard to think of ways to be good to themselves. If it was hard for you to complete the last exercise, or if you want to try something new, read through this list. Here are lots of things that might make your life more fun!

Ways I can be good to my body:
✔ eating healthy, nutritious foods
✔ getting plenty of rest and relaxing
✔ drinking lots of water
✔ playing sports and exercising my body

Ways I can express my creativity:
✔ painting, drawing, making collages
✔ drawing cartoons
✔ crafts, such as making jewelry, painting pottery
✔ taking photos
✔ making a website
✔ sewing, knitting
✔ playing music, writing songs
✔ singing, dancing
✔ writing and illustrating stories and poems

Ways I can exercise my mind:

✔ reading
✔ learning new things
✔ doing schoolwork
✔ solving problems
✔ setting goals
✔ making decisions
✔ daydreaming
✔ role playing

Ways I can connect with others:

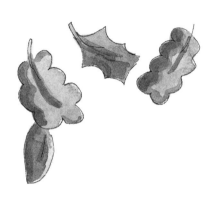

✔ spending time with family and friends
✔ writing letters or telephoning others
✔ emailing my friends
✔ joining an after-school group or sport team
✔ volunteering, helping, and sharing with others
✔ making new friends

LEARNING, PLAYING, AND DOING

All kids need to learn new things, enjoy playing and being with friends, and do lots of fun stuff. Write a list of hobbies, activities, and sports you like to do or would like to learn. Also list any clubs or groups you'd like to join.

1 _____

2 _____

3 _____

4 _____

5 _____

6 _____

7 _____

8 _____

9 _____

10 _____

11 _____

12 _____

13 _____

14 _____

15 _____

16 _____

17 _____

18 _____

Expanding Your Circle of Support

People who study mental health say that the healthiest people have good relationships with friends and family. It helps if we have family and friends around as we're growing up, so we can learn what are called social skills—skills that help us enjoy being with other people, and help us feel safe and happy. Even if you don't have lots of people around, you can build good skills by finding friends who have some of the same interests that you have, such as soccer, art, chess, or swimming.

With different people, you'll have different kinds of friendships. With some people, we may choose to share a lot of ourselves, including our feelings and private thoughts. With other people, we might just like to hang out and share a small part of ourselves. It all depends on what we want in each relationship. You might have lots of hobbies and interests in common with some friends. You probably have just one or two common interests with others, like a favorite video game or team sport. Finding new friends and growing our connections to others is something we do all our lives.

If I wanted to invite someone to be my new friend, here's how I would go about it:

These are some things I would look for in a new friend:

WHO'S IN YOUR HEART?

All of us have people we care about, people we choose to be close to and love. You may also have pets you love and care for, or places and things that are very special to you. Can you think of all the things you care about?

Our hearts usually grow more and more love for others as we go through our lives. Fill the heart to the right with the names of all the people, pets, places, and things you love. Hang a copy of this heart on your wall to help you think about everything you've listed when you feel lonely or sad.

When someone or something new grows in your heart, you can add an extra piece of paper to this heart or draw a new layer around it.

HEART TIES

Maintaining our ties to others is important to our health and happiness!

Fill each of the hearts with the name or drawing of someone you feel connected to, such as a friend or family member.

Being Proud of Yourself

You have the right to feel proud of yourself for all kinds of things, for being a unique person with all your own thoughts, ideas, feelings, and wishes. You have probably done many things that you're proud of. Everyone has different talents, strengths, and other things about them that make them special.

You may even find that your experience with your parent has helped you develop a special strength or talent. You can be proud of that too! For example, lots of kids like you are extra sensitive and kind to others. Also, kids like you are often not bothered by stuff that bothers other people. These strengths can be important sources of pride too.

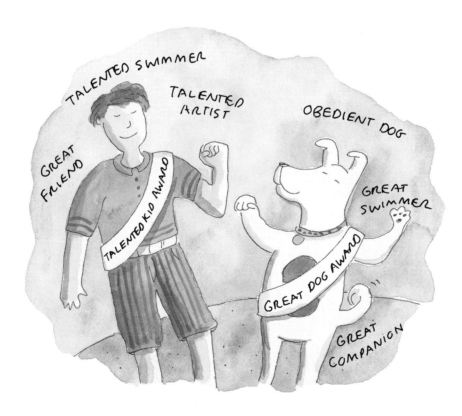

I am proud of myself
for:

My strengths and talents are:

Giving Yourself Credit

Sometimes when you're feeling sad or worried, it may be hard to change your mood and think of good things. You might already know that your thoughts, feelings, and actions are all connected to each other. So the kind of thoughts you dwell on affect your feelings and make them grow. If you think about sad things, for example, your sad feelings will grow.

If you can shift your thinking to something more positive, your feelings and actions will probably follow. One of the ways you can do this is to write yourself a letter or note when you are feeling good about yourself, so that you can read it when you're not feeling quite so good. Your letter should include encouraging thoughts you would tell a friend to cheer them up.

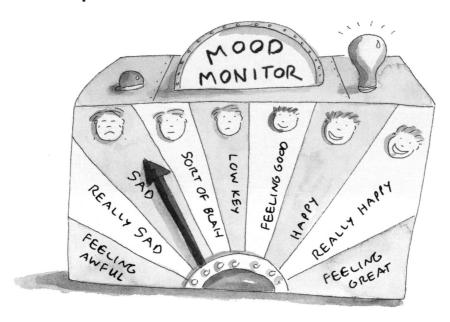

Dear Myself

AFFIRMATIONS

Try writing positive sentences known as affirmations. These are called "I" statements that we can make about ourselves, such as, "I am a capable and smart person" or "I am loved by lots of people." One nice thing you can do for yourself is keep a few written affirmations with you to remind yourself of good thoughts that can help change your mood. You can call these written affirmations "give yourself credit" cards.

Cut out the affirmation cards on the next page, or think of some of your own, maybe with the help of a parent or your therapist or another adult. If you can use a computer, type your affirmations in a small size, print them on heavy paper, and cut them into pieces the size of a credit card.

On the back side of your cards, create your own art. Ask an adult to use a laminator to coat your "give yourself credit" cards in protective plastic, so that they can be stored in your pocket or backpack all the time.

Now, no matter where you go, you'll be able to give yourself a pep talk by reading the messages on your cards.

I AM LEARNING TO RELAX AND HAVE MORE FUN.

I CAN STAND UP FOR MYSELF!

I WISH MYSELF GOOD THINGS ALWAYS.

I AM CONNECTED AND IMPORTANT TO OTHERS.

I PROMISE MYSELF TO DO EVERYTHING IN MY POWER TO MAKE TODAY A GOOD DAY.

IT'S OKAY TO ASK OTHERS FOR HELP WHEN I NEED IT.

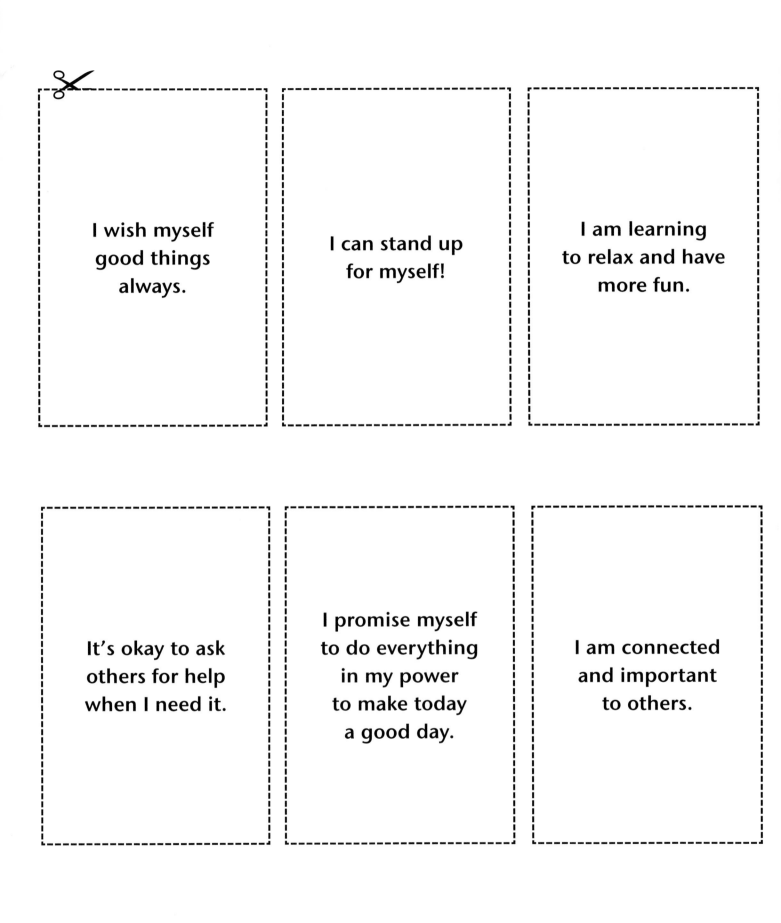

I wish myself
good things
always.

I can stand up
for myself!

I am learning
to relax and have
more fun.

It's okay to ask
others for help
when I need it.

I promise myself
to do everything
in my power
to make today
a good day.

I am connected
and important
to others.

DREAMS FOR MY FUTURE

This is a picture of my dreams for my future.

Draw or write your ideas inside the thought clouds.

If you meet other kids who have just found out that one of their parents has a mental illness, what will you tell them about your experience?

What will you tell them are the most important things you've learned about having a parent with mental illness?

What are the most important things you've learned about yourself?

What other advice would you give to them?

Feeling Proud

Having a parent who struggles with a mental illness can be tough for kids. Reading this book has helped you learn all about mental illness, as well as many ways you can be good to yourself and cope with stress in your life. Talking about your feelings and asking for help or information when you need it is very important to your health and well-being. You can really help yourself out by continuing to use the skills you've learned in this book. And you can feel proud of yourself for keeping at it.

You deserve to feel proud of yourself for completing this workbook. Congratulations! On the next page, you and your helper can fill out the certificate to show what you have accomplished. You may want to post your certificate someplace where it can remind you of what you have learned.

We wish you and your family wellness, always.

OFFICIAL CERTIFICATE OF ACHIEVEMENT

THIS DOCUMENT CERTIFIES THAT

_____
(NAME)

has completed the workbook
WISHING WELLNESS
Congratulations on a job well done!

_____
TODAY'S DATE

ABOUT THE AUTHOR

LISA ANNE CLARKE is a professional child, youth, and
family counselor who specializes in helping families with a parent
suffering from mental illness. An earlier draft of this book,
titled "I Wish You Well Always," was developed by the author as part
of the curriculum for a family outreach program in British Columbia.
Lisa Anne Clarke lives on the west coast of Canada
in Nanaimo, British Columbia.

ABOUT THE ILLUSTRATOR

BONNIE MATTHEWS has illustrated many children's books.
Her whimsical characters have also appeared in more than
100 magazines worldwide, and on gift wrap, greeting cards, tin cans,
and even the cover of the Land's End Kids catalog.
She lives in Baltimore, Maryland.